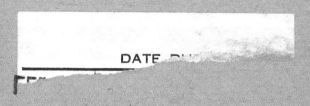

DATE DUE

First U.S. Edition in 1991
published by Boyds Mills Press
A Highlights Company
910 Church Street, Honesdale, PA 18431
Originally published as
NOEL SANS PAROLES
© 1990 by Rainbow Grafics Intl., Brussels
All Rights Reserved.
Library of Congress Catalog Card Number: 90-83430
ISBN 1-878093-08-8
Printed in Portugal.

SILENT CHRISTMAS

Illustrated by Josse Goffin

BOYDS MILLS PRESS

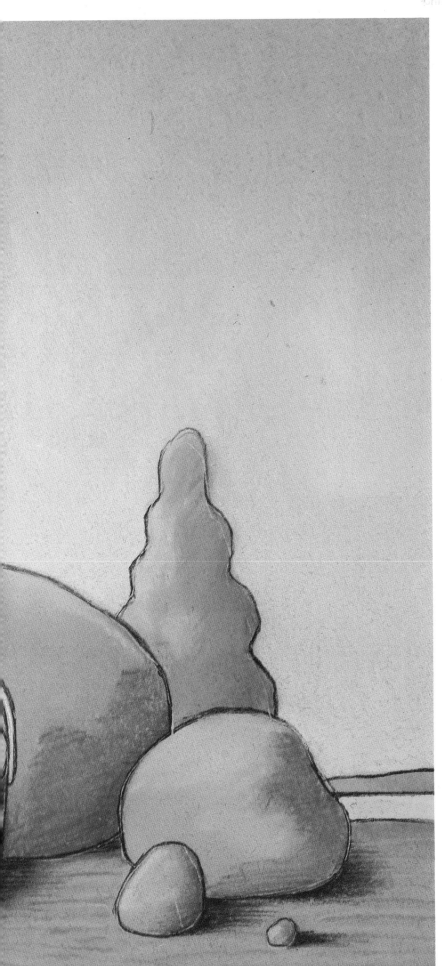

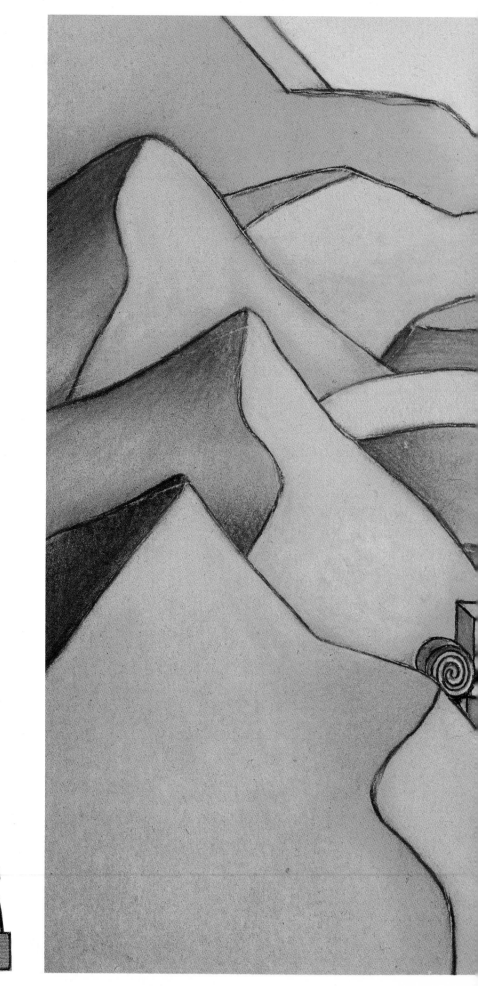

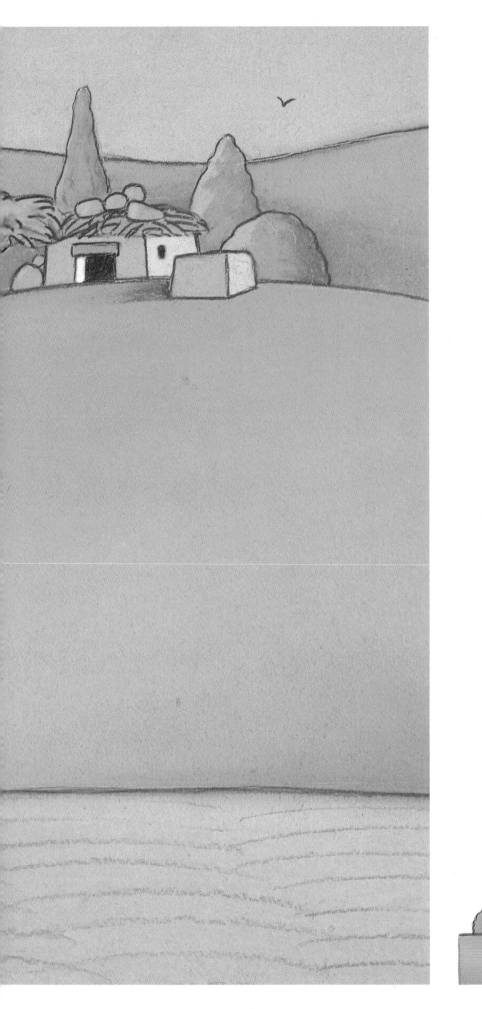

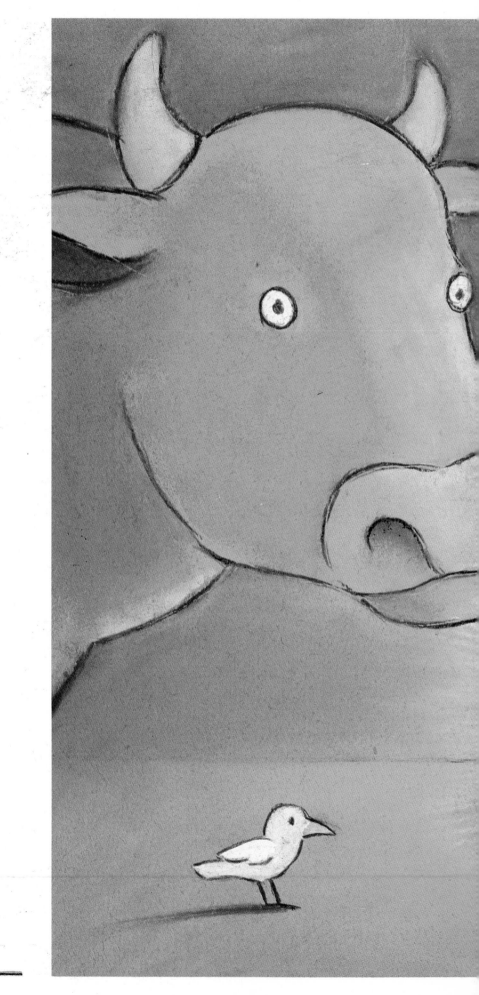

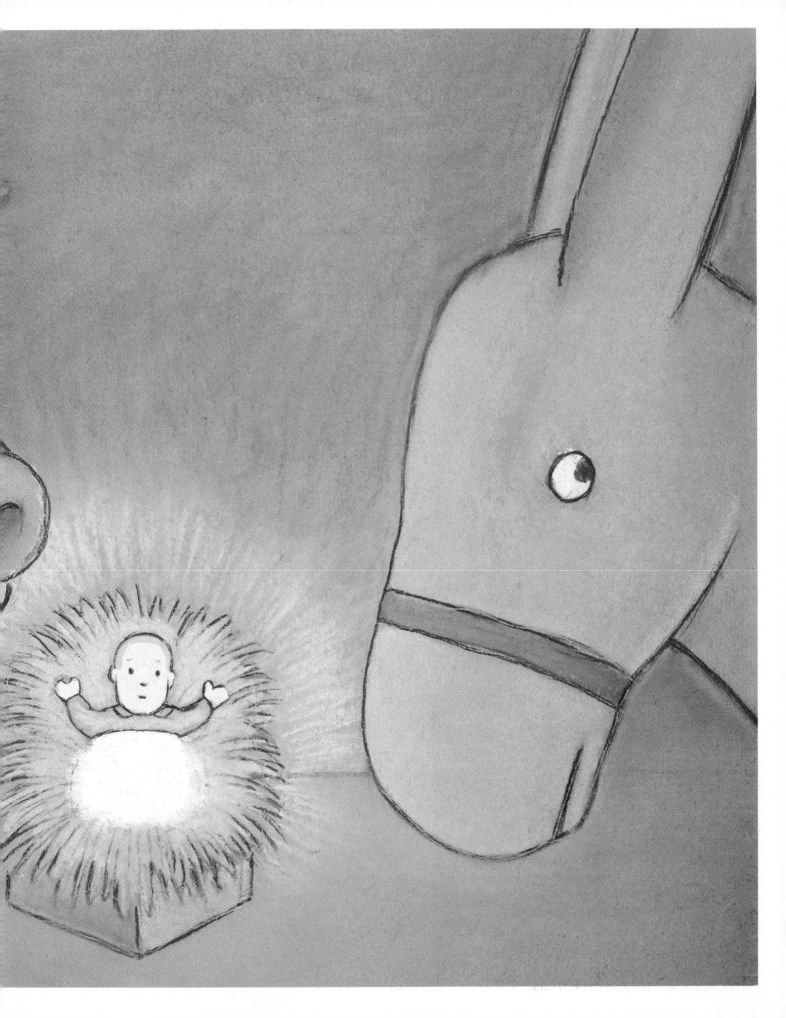